All That in Reeseworth

Written and
illustrated by

Ms Peanut

Published 2024 by Kindle Direct Publishing

This edition published by Notion Press

Story Copyright ©Ms. Peanut

Illustrations Copyright ©Ms. Peanut

To my **friends**, my **parents**, and June.

You guys are awesome and give me such
dazzling ideas, even when you don't try.

I've always wondered what nothing looks
like.

I wonder if nothing looks black and empty.

Or largely blank white.

But I imagine those to be coloured spaces,
and that is *something.*
Which means it isn't nothing.

I've never seen nothing.
Nobody has, by far.

Nothing is a word.
Which says something.

I've felt nothing before.
Or at least I think I have.

It could be called emptiness.
Or loneliness.
I guess they mean 'nothing' in different
situations.

But I have seen nothing in existing spaces.

And you can say there was nothing in my
school locker, either.

Perhaps nothing in my heart, to add.

Ever since we left behind my friends and my home where I'd lived most of my life, I haven't been too cheery.

One would expect to feel sad or excited to move away.
I didn't know *what* to feel.

Did I feel anything?
I don't know. Grey, perhaps?

1 2 3 4 5
BOY
MEETS
BOY

Chapter 1

Kylen

My phone was buzzing like *crazy*. It's awfully annoying, and I was planning to put it on silent soon. My mom always says not to silence it in case of emergencies, but I don't get many calls or texts, emergency or no emergency. *Ever.*

Until now.

On any old weekend in my house, I usually hang out with my friends or stay in to read a good book, write journal stuff, or piece together pictures from my scrapbook.

But ever since I joined the group chat of my three new friends here in Reeseworth, it seemed everyone preferred debating about broccoli being an excellent vegetable online today instead.

I'm still getting used to having company again. It's like reading a new genre or something, seeing that these guys are pretty different from the usual kind. Excluding Beckett. *He's* the usual kind.

I'm barely online in the GC, so I'm flooded by dozens and hundreds of texts, never mind what *day,* what *hour.*

Even when we're at *school.*

Like I said, I only have my phone there for emergencies, and like I said, *never. Happening.*

I mean, yeah, I do have contacts on it. But it's all fun and games only when I'm saving the number of my friends, all smiling excitedly.

Truth is, it's just collecting dust in my list of contacts. They're not going to call, and neither are they going to answer when I do.

Usually I don't, so it's always silent on both sides of the conversation.

And, as usual for the new gang, I was having about twenty-something notifications from the chat.

But it wasn't as annoying when I opened it. The broccoli topic was... actually getting pretty interesting.

PIXIE: aaa guess what im having for lunchhh

PIXIE: It's broccoli of all things!!

One long talk about bogus scam broccolis later

*IDK: I Don't Know. This one is pretty well known.

You guys are bonkers- no offence

BECKETT: We are sorta bonkers, so none taken

VAL: We really have nothing else to talk about huh...

I do have something! If anyone wants to hear, that is

BECKETT: Oh woah, what is it 

It's just that Madilyn Mei has released a new song, and I just found out! It's amazing.

VAL: Oh yeah well that's great haha

*LOL: Laughing Out Loud.
Also well-known.

VAL: Oh! I was looking forward to having a proper chat today. Too bad the most sane one here has to go. It's literal DEATH when you leave us with Pixie 😂

PIXIE: HEY WAT 😆

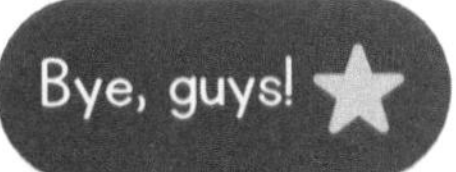

Bye, guys! ⭐

PIXIE: byebye alien 👽

BECKETT: See ya

VAL: Seeya later, alligator

This is the usual conversation in my group chat.

They seem a good bunch, right? Finding nice kids to hang out with is hard, especially for me.

I also knew that my friends didn't entirely get me, but they did accept me all the same, which was lovely of them.

Sitting on my bed, legs crossed, I reread the conversation word by word, over and over.

I could never forget the fact that I was just an addition to the group.

Were they fine without me?

"You are bonkers."

"You're an alien."

"You're different."

Pixie didn't mean what she said. She was just joking. But she was right.

"I am pretty much an alien," I sighed, leaning backwards and flopping on my bed to stare at the ceiling.

My room was tidy due to all the clothes stuffed messily in my closet. I decided I'd save time that way, but unfortunately, my mum disagreed. Shh, don't tell her.

The house was quiet, with Mum out working extra for her new job at a small graphic design company. Hailey, my older sister, was upstairs, studying. She'd gotten into this big school, and she's been doing her best. It was for my mum's new job that we moved here to Reeseworth. Reeseworth is a pretty beach town with vintage cottages built with beautiful architecture. I lived in one of those, too, a much preferable upgrade to my previous old, tattered house, which had way too many space issues.
The beach is good but almost always crowded, and nobody cares to clean up after themselves. Plastic and garbage was always all over the sand. Okay, so the beach isn't exactly the best, but we'll have to do.

I met Val and Pixie at school, and Beckett was my neighbour. Val and I got along quickly because she made it easy for me to talk without going blank. She's a fantastic genius with her guitar skills and brains. I respect anyone who has a passion for music. She's about the third person who's actually genuinely interested in what I have to say (the first being my sister, the second an old friend I don't often contact).

Pixie was just part of Val's package, I guess. She wasn't happy I was the one with all the attention, so she sometimes joined in the conversation, no matter how nerdy. Pixie is not the nicest person ever, though she appears so, but compared to the high-ho intimidating kids in my school, I'll say she is much, much better. She has an obsession with shiny trinkets, beads, accessories and fashion. Pixie would automatically be my best friend if I were interested in any of these. But I mostly wore T-shirts, sweaters, and dark-coloured hoodies to go with my jeans and black pants. Not too appealing to sparkly fluorescent Pixie Waterson.

Beckett was chill and calm, so when I was with him, I became chill and calm, too. I don't know how I just did. My loud thoughts simply block out when he's going on and on about video game lore, comic books and lovely stories about himself (though I wish I could talk more). I like comics and graphic novels, too- video games, not so much, though I make an exception for Sonic the Hedgehog (which Beckett didn't like as much).

My new school was, well, typical. Crazy, fun, *super-terrifying*- the usual. Without Pixie and Val, I don't think I'd have ever survived. Okay, so that would be an exaggeration. I would've survived, but I'd felt like a deer in headlights. I'd experimented with acting 'mysterious' and 'cool' before I'd met them- it really doesn't work in the long run. I just made myself look like an invisible, don't-care-ish kid. I got lonely pretty quickly. Though I didn't like crowds, I liked having friends, but I couldn't call myself a social butterfly because I was *not*.

My house was fantastic- period.
My mom helped me change my room twice, and my bed still couldn't find a good corner to stay put. Shifting furniture is such a hassle, but strangely, I always like the outcome. (But I'd like it if the rearranging was done less often.)

My sister Hailey? She was quite the **star.** When she was my age, she was so carefree and always spoke her mind, contrary to me. She has never lost her shine, and I would have never admitted it, but I was quite jealous of her.

Because what's so interesting about a boring old alien who likes reading oldie stuff? People only notice you if you bother to copy what everyone else likes. You gotta be bright and colourful, a little mature, also largely *immature*... something something.

Maybe I don't find too many friends easily because I never bothered to care about what other kids did like these days.

Chapter 2
Eli

Moving, moving, every year.

I've gotten used to it now, and so has every other kid
whose dad works in the military—in my dad's case,
the **Navy.**
Honestly, making tight friends with anyone is surely a
waste of time, and when you don't have time to
waste, it is impossible. You can say that again.
It is *impossible*.
I'm absolutely tired of moving around our stuff for
the billionth time.
I would be exaggerating about the 'billionth time'. But
still.

I currently don't have any friends- well, any friends
with me right now.
Thing is, I've always been a homeschooler, but don't
come up to me asking if I don't have a single friend. I
do, a lot of them, too. I just haven't found any
meaningful friendship for a long time, two years tops.

But, if I think about it, that was never a problem. I like to be by myself sometimes. A boy needs his me-time from time to time.
I *like* being on my own.

But I also don't.

It depends on my mood.

I keep feeling sad too often. But, look, here's my mom, cheerful ninety per cent of the time, always making friends at the double. All our neighbours are now our family (or so it feels like), and we only got here three weeks ago.

Like I said, not having any friends was never a problem.
It's kind of... becoming a problem.
It's starting to have an effect on me. I feel lonely, and I feel all 'bleugh' - Lonely, lonely aloney loner. Lalalalala.
This is me, Eli Wind, in my room with my sister. Or *'box city',* to be appropriate.
My bedroom walls were usually filled with bookshelves, photos, and cool posters. I typically have to share the room with my younger sister,

TOYS
BOOKS

Elizabeth, who is very messy.

But being a teenager sometimes has its perks. I get to have my own room! No more yelling at Eliza to clean up her books, for goodness sake. No more fighting over what goes where. I'm in charge of my room! I'm on top of the world!
Well.
Not yet. I have yet to unpack for any changes to actually happen. The boxes are all over the house, and I'm not in the mood to do anything. I wish I could just **'abracadabra'** it all into place. Then we could all go to sleep and relax. Some people say 'chillax'. I don't get slang sometimes. It sounds like you're trying to be cool, but you're flat on the ground with an 'I'm stupid' flag.
Get this. People cannot say 'totally' in its whole state anymore. It's 'totes'. 'Obviously' is now 'Obvs'. I do NOT understand why people say **'LOL'** in real life. It was already weird in written form, but I've gotten used to it, and now I'm using it, too, although emojis are enough for me- they're funky.

Gosh, I sometimes wished I had a friend who could keep me company and not nag me all day like my sister.

A friend who'd understand me and listen to me.

But either my friends back at my old home didn't bother to call me back or didn't save my number, so there's no hope there.

Ahhh, what a dream, what a delusion.
It's not like it's gonna happen, anyway.

Every friend I make is just going to disappear one day.
We'll be moving again in the blink of an eye.

(Also, my sister is a good friend and listener, but she's too small to be told big things, you think?)

Chapter 3

Kylen

VAL: Heya gang, meet up at park?

What for?

VAL: to hang out lol

PIXIE: WOAW WHAT TIMEE

VAL: 5ish? When are you free?

PIXIE: 5 sounds good

VAL: @Beckett @Beckett

BECKETT: What

VAL: Hangout at the park around 5 pm. You in?

BECKETT: Ya

PIXIE: @Kale You coming bro ?

5 o'clock seems okay. I'm in.

PIXIE: Bro, sometimes your completely grammatical texts creep me out

Huh?? Why??

I smiled, putting down my phone.

They are soo nice. Oh, well, except for Pixie, who could be a bit sting-y. Okay, so a 'bit' would be an understatement. But she's usually joking, so I'll put her on the nice list. (Ho, ho, ho. Don't call me Santa Claus, mind you.)

But the hard part was asking my mom.
It wasn't often I asked her to go out to hang out with my friends. I wasn't sure how this would go.

She's a good sport, I told myself. *The worst she could say is no.*
The worst she could say was *no.* I winced.

I inched behind my mom, fiddling with my fingers uncertainly. *She could say no. She could say no...*
Shut up, I told myself. *Go, ask her. So what if she said no? You could stay home and be alone or finish a few pages of your scrapbook.*

I sighed and walked to my mom, who was sitting at the dining table, reading a romance novel. It had her *'Kyra's personal library'* sticker on its spine. It was from her personal library, currently in our living room.

"Mom... uh, could I go to the park with my friends at around five?"
Oh, wow, I didn't even have the pluck to ask that I wanted to be there at *precisely* five. Not *around* five.

"Sure, Kaley," she smiled, looking up from her yellowed *Sophie Kinsella* copy. That's my nickname. Kaley, based on the plant, Kale. "When do you plan to be back?"

Oh, right- I didn't get that cleared.

"Oh, uh, around seven? Ish?" I shrugged.

"Okay, dear. Take your phone with you, and call me in case anything happens. Be back before it gets too dark." Mom patted me.

Yeah, yeah- be safe, don't go in the dark, be good- the usual. I know.

I didn't tell her that. I nodded and muttered something about getting ready.

She said yes.

Okay, so should I have been *happy* or *upset* that I couldn't do my SCRaPBooK today?

Agh, the backup plan actually sounded better than the original plan.

Okay, now I had to decide what to wear. This was utterly and simply one of life's biggest problems.

"Wear the ol' T-shirt and jeans combo, man,"

No, that would be a problem, too, because I wear only two pairs of jeans, mostly at school, and wearing them now would make everyone think I *had* only two pairs *ever.* Perhaps I was overthinking this. But it kept bugging me like a broken record going over and over again.

So eventually, I opened the closet of *Old and Random Things Not Used Very Often.*
Old jeans… new jeans… Ahh, man, these wouldn't do.

"Why can't I just be normal and *pick* something, for goodness sake?" I sighed heavily, tugging at my hair on one side.
I decided to wear a new pair I'd been unsure of. It was slightly loose, so I had to tug it up now and then.
I wanted to wear my favourite turtleneck sweater, but I put it back with a sigh, as I'd already worn it the last time we'd hung out. And the time before that.
Rejected, rejected, rejected, rejected…
Soon, my bed was covered with a dozen shirts turned inside out, all no-gos.
Ah, who am I kidding? I gotta wear something.

I wore a plain, dark, camo T-shirt. It's not a hundred per cent satisfactory, but the clock is ticking. I glare at it. Time probably hates me since I have never used it like a normal person.

Ten minutes left to five. Wow, good timing.

I got on my tattered yellow bicycle and sped through the warm neighbourhood. I could hear the waves crashing away in the distance- seriously, they were that loud, plus the beach wasn't too far.
I loved the houses in this town- they're so lovely and vintage, worn down around the edges, but so green and pretty all the same.

I live in one of them. I still couldn't believe it- it was too good to be true, kinda.
I loved my new house, but it still felt foreign to me- according to my head, we were just here on holiday, and one day, we would be back in our old house. Unfortunately, reality didn't agree. I felt like a void of emptiness, like a hole, had just started growing within me, where everything used to be.

How can leaving behind a house and a couple of friends make you feel heavy with lumps in your throat?

As I passed my school road, I blinked rapidly. I think I had something in my eye. But I went on.

Soon, I was nearing the park entrance. I parked my cycle near a bunch of others, locking it up. I stuffed the key, along with its Sonic-themed keychain, into my pocket. I then started to rub my eyes roughly.

Aghh. I can't cry now. I gulped down a large dollop of water to wash off the lump in my throat, but it just made it worse.

I drank half the bottle.

Ping!

A notification from the group chat. Speak of the devil- or angels, maybe, more suitably.

It was from Val.

Ky, you're coming, right?

I smiled weakly and typed a reply.

Yep, I'm here parking my bike

We see you! Look up

I looked up. My friends were waving frantically with bright faces. I waved back weakly.

"Ky, come over here! Quick!" Pixie called out in her bubbly voice. Everyone was sitting together on a polka-dotted mat spread over the grass.
Pixie had brought her classic bead tin, decorated with tiny beads to make **flowers**. She was known for making bracelets and anything to do with beads and thread.
I've heard from Val that her mom owns a small boutique across town, which makes sense.

It never crossed my mind that we could bring things along. I winced, wishing I'd thought of bringing my scrapbook.
I plopped down with them a bit rougher than I'd intended. *Oof.*

"Hiya, what are you guys doing?" I asked, put off by the fact that I wasn't in the loop. I mean, they were there before me somehow, which looked pretty odd.

"I'm not sure," Val shrugged casually. "Pixie's found herself something to do, that's for sure,"
Pixie frowned indignantly. "Oh, yeah, sorry, I thought of something to actually do, unlike you guys,"
Val laughed but paused when she saw me dully fiddling with the grass.

"Ky, you okay?" she asked with a concerned expression.

I perked up. I put on an enthusiastic voice, smiling. "Sure, I'm fine!"

Not.

"You look a little dull. You sure you're okay?" Beckett put in.

Oh, goodness, if they asked anything further, I might've started to break.

"I-I'm okay! Just a little tired," I wave my hand for effect, chucking nervously. "Well, since all of us are bored, maybe we can talk about any of our latest happenings," I suggested, hoping they'd let it go if I changed the subject.

"Our latest… happenings?" Pixie raised an eyebrow.

"Y'know, interesting stuff that happened most recently to you, if you get what I mean," I blabbered.

"Well, my cousin's getting married next week, and my mom says we gotta go," Val said.

Pixie nodded knowingly as I stopped smiling.

Val glanced at Beckett expectantly, motioning him to talk.

"Oh, I'm going to Walesbury to see this new film based on Dart Prozone," Beckett grinned.

Dart Prozone was a video game made about fifteen

years ago about a kid called Dart who has lightning bolt powers and owns an old race car passed down from generations. I don't know more about the game lore since it's all just bashing around with race cars. It's not like it was made for storytelling purposes anyway. I don't care for it much because of that reason.

"Wow, *Walesbury*," I wondered aloud. "That's pretty far away… are you going there just 'cause you wanted to see the film or…?" I couldn't go to a big city simply because I wanted to watch a movie, and I couldn't imagine Beckett's parents letting him either, as strict as they were.

"Of course not," Beckett shook his head. "My mom's taking me there to see this science exhibit and some other stuff- book fairs and whatnot," Beckett sighed, crossing his legs.
"That sounds like something I would enjoy, actually," I laughed. Beckett laughed, too, but Pixie glared at me in disbelief. I stopped laughing.

But I'd just realised something.

"You… you guys are leaving?" I blinked.

"Just for the week," Val gently patted me.

"I'll be gone for two weeks, actually," Beckett shrugged. "My parents have got some business in the city, meeting some officers and everything," Beckett's dad worked in the Navy, so his family leaving for work wasn't a new thing. And school was out for the month, anyway.

That meant the only friend available was Pixie. A speck of a chance I was going to hang out with her. She was fine and all, but she didn't really see me as a significant friend. As far as I know, anyway.
I was going to be alone. For three weeks, I was by myself. It sounded the equivalent of crickets chirping in the desert.

"Hey," Val smiled softly, snapping me back. "Don't worry; at least we have two more weeks to spend together,"
"Oh, yeah," I brightened up. "I forget,"
"And I'll have a week left to hang with you guys," Beckett grinned.
"Right," I smiled. Pixie wasn't as bright since nobody was looking at her.

I have to admit, we're an awkward group (Okay, if you

rule out Pixie. She's confident, bubbly, and straightforward, and is also friends with half her school), but we're a tight bunch.

But sometimes, I wondered why I still felt a sort of void within me if I had such good friends to fill it.

Chapter 4

Eli

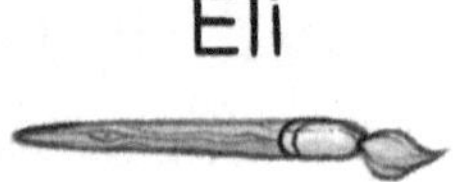

Okay, so unpacking isn't as easy as it seems.

Neither is packing, especially when your dad isn't around, and it's just you, your mom, and packers who speak a different language. It doesn't help that I can only manage when I need to answer a 'yes' or 'no' question—I'm not very fluent in Spanish.

Because of my horrible Spanish, I ended up packing my books and art supplies alone. To be honest, I preferred it that way since the stuff would be easy to unpack and set up. But it would've taken less time if I could tell the packer people what exactly had to be done. Some boxes were stuffed up at random.

A couple of things didn't make it, and we were still weeping over this broken trophy my dad had preserved for almost twenty-five years.

My dad has a very big passion for sports.
Back in his school days, he played all the sports you
can think of- basketball, volleyball, badminton, tennis,
hockey, and so on. He was known for being the best
sportsman in his school. But more than anything,
hockey had his heart. He'd always wanted to be a
hockey player but didn't make the cut, becoming a
Navy officer instead.

When I was younger, I didn't care much for sports.
But when my peers asked me why I never tried, it
made me think. So, before we'd moved, I'd asked my
parents if I could try out a sport. They agreed and
asked me what I wanted to try, and I went with
basketball as hockey wasn't taught there, to my dad's
dismay.

I made quite a number of friends in my basketball
class rather quickly, but I knew once I moved, they
wouldn't find time to keep in touch. And my life
would start over again with a new house, new friends,
and a new place- the loop doesn't end anytime soon.
And once I move, I'll adjust to the new place as
quickly as possible, the frequent contact with old
friends slowly fading away, again and agan.
I'm sure it's going to be the same *here*, too.

I know there's nothing I can do about it- I can't help that my dad has a transferable job. And I've lived this way for a long time, and you can guess I'm used to it by now.

But, recently moving house all over the country doesn't seem as colourful anymore. In fact, I feel more of a dark grey. Normally I feel something like 'yellow' or 'orange'.
Friends are getting harder to make, and I can feel myself outgrowing things I loved when I was younger. I can't draw a single good picture- every line and stroke doesn't have that energy in it. My work suddenly looks so hard to me, and the words start to fly off the page, everything looking gibberish. I don't like this feeling. When I write it all down, it just sounds like I'm a soggy grump of a cat, unhappy with life. But it helps to pour it down somewhere.

The only thing that's kept my spirits up is decorating my new room. I decided to clear off all the random boxes in my room whenever I felt in a rut. Mom, Eliza, and I are currently staying in the VIP suite in the officers' mess.

A month before we packed to leave Aurefields, my

dad had already left for Reeseworth, leaving us to handle unfinished business. He planned to take a few days off to help us, but his request was declined.

The three of us came here to Reeseworth by flight, carrying three suitcases, two backpacks, and two handbags all by ourselves.
Eliza coped really well to our convenience. Her plushie bunny, Floppy, was given most of the credit for her good behaviour- Eliza doesn't go anywhere without her dear Floppy. You should have seen her face when I took her out of my backpack before we boarded the plane. She was so sad when we had to pack her because Floppy was prone to getting lost (we left her in two restaurants, a friend's house, and a garment store, *all* in the same month we got her).

Also, I'm so glad I didn't flinch when she went on about being hungry on the plane. Not sure how it would've gone if I gave her my secret stash of jelly fruit squares when she buggered me nonstop.

During the three-hour flight, I felt my heart pang. I suddenly realised I had *really* left my old home, emptied of all the life that was in it, with only a layer of dust left behind. I'm not usually one for sentiments, but maybe it was because I was older and my memories were fresher and stronger, I felt like I was absorbed in it.

And then, as I watched the bags spin through the conveyor belt for the third time, I saw my dad. Everything I'd worried about didn't matter anymore-okay, I'd worried that our bags might get left behind, so that worry made an exception.

I was all smiles, not a thing else in my head. As Eliza jumped into my dad's arms, I trailed behind my crying mum. I felt like I wanted to cry myself, but not a tear came out. I don't want to admit it, but I did try to cry-sometimes crying feels nice and warm. I watched Eliza and Mum snuggle into a big hug, as I smiled widely, probably like an idiot.

You know the saying that goes something like, 'You only know the importance of someone when they're not with you'. I really felt that. I hadn't seen my dad for forty days, and I'd never guessed I'd be this happy to see him again. (I don't miss him too much in shorter periods of time.)

In the car, the three of us went on and on about what

he'd missed and how much *we* missed him, filling him in with stories of saying goodbye to neighbours, friends, and the Navy Welfare and Wellness Association (NWWA) members, and about how Mum and I managed to pack all our stuff alone.

I felt all warm and fuzzy inside, not minding the fact that I didn't get to talk as much as I wanted because I had the *whole* day to spend with my dad.

He's incredible, though he doesn't get me sometimes. I doubt if he remembers things about me, such as my favourite show- most likely, he thinks I still like *Dora the Explorer*- but does that really matter, silly stuff like that?
"Dad, Dad, you know that girl called Lenna in basketball class who's always in a good mood and talks to me half the time? She cried as soon as I told her I was moving away, the poor thing,"

"Ed, the packers and movers didn't even bother to bubble-wrap the glass items until I insisted they open up the boxes and do it again properly,"

"Daddy, Daddy, did you know a man packed my glasses while I took them off to nap?"

He listened patiently under the condition that Eliza and I took turns. He couldn't keep track of all my mates, though, so I had to describe them again. But I did make him laugh, all the same.

We'd all woken up at around four o'clock that morning to reach the airport at five and board the plane at six. So, by the time we reached Reeseworth Airport, our energy had sunk to level one. And soon, Eliza was out cold. I lasted for an hour, and then I dozed off as well. The journey from the airport to our new house took around four hours, arriving at lunchtime.

Now we're here, staying in the Officer's Mess, taking a lunch break between unpacking.

Our new house was outside the Navy's residential campus as there weren't any vacant houses to move into. This was a big change for me since I've only remembered living in a white and navy-blue home all my life. The Officer's Mess was in the campus, so I had a couple of good walks in there.
I don't know anyone there and I still don't know my way around, so I usually walked with my dad.
But now he's gone sailing, so, well.

How about my new house, you ask? Well, it was nice.
Instead of the usual navy blue and white paint on the
exterior walls, the cottage was painted in earthy tones,
slightly faded, giving it a vintage appearance.
Little table roses grew wildly in multiple colours in the
small front yard (which we don't get in our quarters
often). We didn't have a terrace; we just had aged
terracotta roofing, which I preferred. I liked vintage
stuff, like the pretty pictures you see on Pinterest.
The neighbouring houses were newly built, making
our old and sturdy one stand out.

But if you'd gone out into the main road a little away
from our street, the houses get older the farther you
went.

But looking around ours, there was a line of *new*
houses. Perhaps it'd been nicer to have oldie houses
around instead of the usual kind.
But, besides that, the neighborhood looked like a great
painting subject.
I thought of my sketchbooks and Posca Pens in our
room, wishing I could have a sketching session right
here.

But I'm pretty sure I've got time for that later on.

But there's this one house across the street that I'm excited to paint more than any other- the only other vintage house on the street.
It was a sunny yellow and had a balcony on its first floor. Vines and flowers grew wildly on its wood railings, hanging a foot below. A tattered old yellow bicycle and a teal Vespa were parked in the front yard. The garden had funky square shrubs, all brightly green.
I wondered who lived in such a pretty house. I was sorta jealous of their home being more vibrant than our earth-coloured one, and the bicycle added a lovely touch.

I could drop the idea of painting the entire line of houses and just paint that yellow one. Overambitious projects weren't my thing just yet- I've learnt that the hard way.

I've got two things to look forward to: setting up my room and painting the yellow cottage.
It looked like things were looking up.

Chapter 5

Kylen

So…

Val and Beckett are supposed to leave this week.

I think that I might cry. (Shh. Don't tell.)
Mom and Hailey aren't looking any less busy, and I
feel like I might burst.
So I did something.
I invited Beckett, Val, and Pixie to my house this
evening. I might as well explain it to you in detail.
We'd all planned to watch a movie, which was simple
enough. It was hard to agree on anything else, anyway.
No matter what we planned, at least *somebody* didn't
feel it was fun.

I was the only one in when Val suggested we make song lyrics together, so that plan was cut, too.
Mom was free for the day since it was a Saturday, but 'free' would be a false statement, seeing as she was flooded with calls anyway, and I could tell she was on a deadline for some project.

So dinner was on Hailey tonight. Simple stuff, really. Hailey kindly offered to make us mustard sandwiches with cheese and vegetables. Even I could have made it myself, but y'know, I wanted to spend time with my friends.

My friends love Hailey. She's cool, she's smart, she's funny, she's lovely- much, much more interesting than me. Sometimes, I get pangs of jealousy out of nowhere when I hear them laughing together. They're my friends, not hers. She already has friends. Why should she come in?
But, yeah, I know, I can't say that. It's unkindly. She didn't do anything wrong. But next to her, I seem like a mess.

I love her so much, but sometimes, don't you ever feel that you want to shut someone up in a cupboard now and then? Even if you'd never actually do it?
I sound like a hateful mouse. Even if I said, '*No, no, I would never think of actually doing such a thing*', it wouldn't change much since I do sometimes imagine that.

So when Hailey answered the door as I was setting up my room, I felt some pull of sorts in me. They were

giggling together when Hailey said something witty. I
was upstairs, peeking over the wooden staircase
handrail in the alleyway. A little annoying voice in my
head went, haha, look, your sister took away your
friends without even trying.

But I knew I was being silly. Of course, she wasn't.
She'd never do that to me. They were still my friends.
They cared enough to bother about me- enough to
chat and want to hang out with me. Me, of all people.
The alien. I'm worth bothering about.
That thought was enough to cheer me up.

"Hi, guys!" I waved from up. Everyone turned
around and waved like crazy. Hailey said something I
couldn't hear, and they all nodded and rushed
upstairs. I felt the excitement get to me.

"KYY!" Val grinned, strolling behind Pixie, who
tripped herself up the stairs in haste.
Beckett came up slower than these two in a more
dignified manner, laughing at Pixie as she picked
herself up.
"Ha, ha, ha," she folded her arms in mock annoyance.
"Ahh, Ky, your bedroom is amazing! It's full of
BOOKS! Oh, and you have Alice Oseman's books,

now, huh?" Val chirped when she spotted my wall shelf of the author's works. I turned slightly red.

"Ahh, yeah, you spotted that already?" I grinned shyly.

"The books look much better in your room than in the living room! Are they all yours?" she gabbled cheerily, running her hands over the books.

"Well, some are hand-me-downs from Hailey and my mom, but mostly, yeah,"

Pixie flopped on the bed, hanging her dainty sling bag on the corner of it. "Your bed is comfy, dude!"

"Still no PS5, hm, Kale?" Beckett nudged me playfully.

"You know I'm never going to get one," I rolled my eyes with a laugh.

"You should. You wouldn't regret it, I tell you,"

"Nuh-uh, no way,"

"Not worth the effort, Beckett. You know it's not gonna work. Video games and Ky simply don't mix. I'll tell you that for free," Val joked, looking away from my Alice Oseman collection.

"Just because I like Sonic doesn't mean I like video games, Beckett," I put in, nudging him playfully.

Beckett made himself comfy on my beanbag, I sat at

my desk with the chair facing them, and Val sat with Pixie.

"Sooooo, about that movie…" Pixie stretched, swinging her legs.

"Yeah?" I tilted my head.

"When are we watching it?"

"As soon as Hailey's done with the snacks,"

"What movie are we watching?" Beckett asked after staring at my Sonic posters with disapproval.

Val looked up from my copy of Solitare, looking at the ceiling for ideas. "Ehh, yeah, what are we watching?"

"It's still not decided. It's up to you guys," I said.

Everyone got their thinking caps on.
Beckett suggested Marvel. I was okay with that as long as it had to do with Spider-Man, but Val and Pixie weren't so keen.
Pixie suggested an anime film, but Beckett was so not on board.
Val suggested a Korean film, but nobody agreed.
I suggested a Disney film, and everyone felt that it wasn't too bad of an idea.
So we got together to watch WALL-E. I'd already seen that film, but it appealed to everyone so much

that we went for it anyway.
And I'll tell you one thing: the movie was far more beautifully written and animated than I remembered. I did watch it as a little kid, anyway.

Then my mom came into the room and greeted everyone with a friendly 'Hallo' and asked us what we'd been doing and everything.

Then she asked us if we'd taken any pictures.
Gosh. No, we hadn't. How could I have forgotten?

Val and I exchanged glances, knowing how much my mom insisted on taking pictures.
"Oh, um, yes, Mrs Scotts," Val lied. "I'll send them over later,"
My mom nodded approvingly and waved goodbye to everyone. I gave her an uneasy grin before she closed the door.

"KY!! THE SNACKS ARE READY!" came a call from downstairs.
Val and Beckett glanced at each other and at me.
"Ky, can I go get them?" Val asked.
"Yeah, sure?" I blinked in confusion.
"I'm going with her," Beckett rushed to the door and

gave us a quick wave before disappearing.

I'm guessing they were hungry.

So now I was alone in my bedroom with Pixie on my
bed, twirling her hair absentmindedly, staring at the
wall. There wasn't anything there to interest her. She
was swinging her legs at a fast pace and looked
twitchy.

I made the fan a bit faster since the room was pretty
hot. That's the problem- I'm used to hot climates, but
only a few here like the heat. And when I did, I
accidentally turned off the lights. Pixie gasped. I
laughed. I made a ghost noise, which creeped her out
more.

"AHH, Ky!" she squeaked.

"Pff- sorry," I grinned.

"Hmph,"

I turned on the fairy lights on my table and glanced at
Pixie, who looked really like a pixie in the soft,
mellow lighting. I found myself reaching for my small
Canon camera in my drawer, but I put it back since I
remembered it was off limits until next week because
I'd spilt chocolate milk all over one of Hailey's
textbooks. I did get told off very badly for that. So I
took my phone instead.

Pixie eyed me curiously as I moved, so I walked

rather awkwardly across the room to pick up my
phone.

"Hey, Pixie, look up," I clicked a picture of her
looking surprised.

"Hey, what was that?" Pixie folded her arms in mock
annoyance.

"Hold still, silly," I laughed and tried to take a better
photograph, but Pixie started swaying side to side.

"Pixie!"

"Na-na-na-na,na," she taunted and
giggled.

I sighed in defeat and looked at the
pictures.

"Pixie… they've all come out shaky," I groaned, but they all came out so funny and weird, making me laugh again. "They're all so silly. It's like you're a… a ghost!"

"Ha. Ha. How funny," Pixie rolled her eyes, chuckling.

Just then, I had an idea.

"Pixie! You're bored, aren't you?"

"Hm? I guess, yeah," she shrugged.

"Why don't we make a ghost movie together?"

"A… ghost movie?"

"Yeah! You can star in it!"

"As… the ghost?" she raised an eyebrow in annoyance.

"That's… yet to be decided," I grinned uneasily, unable to decode her dead expression.

But then she laughed.

Beckett and Val came into the room, munching on something.

"*Mm-mm-mm,* why didn't you guys come downstairs to eat maple syrup bananas?" Beckett asked after swallowing his banana. "And why are the lights off?"

"We're going to make a ghost movie," I said enthusiastically.

"Wait, we're actually going with this idea?" Pixie

snarked.

Val grinned. "Wowie, sounds fun! Who's the ghost?"

It was me.

I was cast as the ghost.

Hey. Don't laugh, it's not funny. I was the only one with the appropriate hair.

Pixie had the longest out of all of us- but her locks were blonde. She was better off playing Barbie or Rapunzel.

Beckett's brown hair is the shortest.

Val's is a dark bob.

And my hair is dark brown, the second longest. I plan to cut it soon.

Long story short, we did not finish the film. It was around nine when they left, and we had more *bloopers* than actual footage. Besides, we couldn't hear a single word in the video even though we all spoke far too loudly. But, y'know something?

That was the most fun I'd had in days.

And, maybe one day, I'll get to know Pixie more.

She's still a mystery, snarky one moment and bubbly the other.

Or *maybe* I'm better off not knowing.

Chapter 6

Kylen

This morning, my mom sent me to the supermarket to get a packet of noodles. Hailey said she was too swamped to go.

Thank goodness I'd checked myself in the mirror before heading out. My hair was a crow's nest, and my eyes were still crusty.

I prayed to no one in particular that I should not mess up today.

I pulled on my sneakers with the done laces and pulled the door open. Phew. Nobody was around. I locked the latch. No, I wasn't locking my family away– they could always come through the back door. And when I turned around, I saw her.

That tall girl with pretty hair and a gentle voice. She was talking to someone gaily on her phone.

She'd talked to me like that before but never truly

meant it.
She was just being nice.
But she's not.

I ran back into my house until she was gone.
Her name's <u>Shanelle Heywood.</u>

My friends despised her, but Pixie wavered between under her charm.

What baffled me was that she was so kind and helpful when I first met her at school. But she would slip in a remark about me here and there to everyone else. I can't believe how fast I fell for the pretentious act.
I'm so glad school's out, and I don't need to see Shanelle every day in my

face (although I knew she wouldn't *eat* me or whatever). I've got Val and Pixie now, I don't think it will happen again, maybe.

But there she was, right out in front of the fencing, in her teal crop top and flare jeans, on her phone with dainty fingers.

Go away, I chanted in my head. *Go away, go away, go away…*

I spied through the doorhole, watching her walk casually on the sidewalk, away and away, ever so slowly. Did she have to take so long?

She did go, eventually.

I sighed in relief. I could step out freely now. Just had to stay clear of chatty people and anyone who knew me. I feel like I was bicycling in a war zone. *Hey, look, a freak, free to jeer at. He won't mind too bad, surely.*

My mom said it was all in my head. My books said I had to be myself. My friends said I'm great the way I am. I knew I shouldn't hate myself so easily. But I do, I do, sometimes, even if I have no good reason to.

I sped faster. The supermarket wasn't too far, now.

I parked my bicycle beside most others in front of the two-storeyed store.

REESEWORTH SUPERMARKET.

I ambled inside and hoped no soul would know me. I should only be known as the Mysterious Random Kid. Not Ky Scotts, the idiot who lives a couple of streets away.

The Boy Who Blubbers,
The Mouse Who Squeaks,
The Weird Kid Who Knows of Nothing.

I spotted the spaghetti section. I walked as casually as possible towards it, but a man was in the way, checking out some mustard seeds. I pretended to be very interested in the nearby curry powder. Ah, yes, curry powder and all the ingredients that went in it. Aha, and also, it expires in three months…

Finally, he walked away, and I sighed in relief— noodles at last. I reached for one in the back as my mother said that was where the recently manufactured packs were kept. All I had to do was to pay super quick and then leave-
CRASH.
All the noodle packs tumbled down, and everyone around me stared.
Ha, great.
"Sorry," I mumbled and frantically picked them up in

fives with both my hands.

I didn't look away from what I was doing in case I made awkward eye contact with anyone. Finally, I put everything back, including the one I was about to buy. Shoot.

I took a random one and strolled to the billing counter. Did the left arm swing with the left leg? No, no, that's not how human beings walked…

I stood behind the small queue of grownups with their shopping. Phew, they all had a small load of stuff to bill. I didn't have to wait long. I distracted myself by looking at a couple of kids outside the glass-walled supermarket.

They were laughing.

I imagined their relationship. Maybe they were the best of friends.

Perhaps they weren't.

They might have fought a lot or not at all.

Perhaps one was always left out, or all were equal.

They could have been enemies once or maybe one day in the future.

Maybe not.

They might grow up together or split up midway.

They may have been once childhood friends, or they only met recently.

Perhaps they were friends only because they liked the same show, or-

"Kid?"
AGH. I was holding the line.
"Sorry, Maisy," I awkwardly plopped the noodle packet on the counter.
"Where's your head at, hm?" she asked teasingly as she scanned.

BEEP.

"Sorry, Maisy. I… my head… I'm just, y'know, kinda… sleepy?" I blubbered.
"Pff, I see," she rolled her eyes with a chuckle. "It's always 'Sorry, Maisy' and no other answer, huh?"
I zipped my mouth. *Shut up. Please shut up.*
I paid with fumbling fingers.
"With long fingers like that, you could become a pianist or something," Maisy joked.
"Huh?" I blinked.
She sighed heavily. Maybe she thought I was dense. Perhaps I *was* dense. I probably didn't have any friends because of that, and I should really work on my-
"You're holding the line, kid,"

"Oh! Sorry, Maisy,"

"Just… just go,"

You don't know how fast I rode home that day. Maybe my friends were always going to be ahead of me. I can't even do *shopping* without feeling out of place.

Chapter 7

Eli

My mom said I was spending *WAY* too much time in my room and that I had to go out for a walk, and I felt this was the perfect opportunity to sketch that yellow house.

I'll tell you one thing for sure—drawing while balancing a sketchbook on a wooden fence is harder than it looks. The grass was damp that evening since it had been pretty drizzly earlier, so the ground wasn't the best place to sit.
It was nice and breezy, and I was totally into the sketch. By now, my pencil had a dozen bite marks on it. The house was pretty complex, and the fence made a terrible table.
I don't know how, but the sketch came out kinda great. I have those moments where I make a masterpiece, but I could never make another one like that again. It just happens. It's so annoying that I can never figure out how to do the same thing again.

And when a boy came out of the house, looking at what I was doing, I panicked, but then I realised I wasn't really doing anything wrong.

He seemed pretty awkward at first, especially with how he stood and bit his lip, but he waved to me in a friendly way. I waved back, closing my sketchbook instinctively.

Goodness me, it can be very embarrassing when you're looking for that one page in a sketchbook full of bad, kiddie and embarrassing drawings. I love what I draw, but it's not for everyone. People can be rather judgemental, and I don't always feel like dealing with it.

He asked me what I was doing there so often in front of his house, going straight to the point. I fumbled through my sketchbook, asking him to come and see my picture. He was very chill about it, and he actually liked it.

Wow, not a single bad remark. I got pretty excited and explained how I constructed his house in my sketch. I didn't go too far—I sometimes sound like a boring chatterbox. BUT when I saw his face properly, I recognised him immediately.

I don't know how I came five minutes into the conversation without even figuring out who it was??

After he told me his name, I thought, *This does it! How did I not recognise him?*

And when I introduced myself, he knew who *I* was, too.

Oh. My. Goodness. I could, like, never find a way to express how much I'd missed him.

I felt like jumping up and down like a little kid. But I didn't. I just stood there, staring at him like an idiot. I think I scared him, though, the way he bit his lip again.

Okay, so I wanted to write this bit as if it were the most beautiful reunion in the history of friendship, but no, I do *not* have the ability to. No matter how detailed I write it, it will always sound bad, and it wasn't all so magic-ky anyway.

We were just standing there in deadpan silence. I mean, what were the odds of meeting your childhood best friend, who coincidentally lived on the same street? Out of the blue? Awkward silences are to be expected.

I gave him a stupid grin.

He grinned back.

I grinned wider.

I giggled.

He giggled.

"It's been so long, dude," I said, hugging my sketchbook.

"It has. Three years, right?" Ky replied.

"Well, yeah. And we've been friends for what, four years or something?" I said, tapping on my fingers one by one.

"That's a long time, huh?"

"Pretty much,"

"So, how's things lately?" Ky asked awkwardly.

"Uh, pretty good. I live a way off in that street over there," I pointed.

"Oh, wow, that's awesome!" he gasped. "You live so nearby, I can just, like, *walk* over,"

"Ah, yeah, right, you can!" I beamed.

"Wait, don't you usually live in a quarters or something?" Ky asked, letting me inside his front yard.

"I do, yeah, but all the buildings were occupied, so we had to move in outside it,"

"Well, then. This is great," Ky grinned ear to ear.

"This is," I replied, tousling my hair on one side.

"How long you been here?"

"Three weeks, tops,"

"I've been here a couple of months. More than four,"

"Then you must know your way around, right?" I asked.

"Yeah, I kinda do, but I'm still forgetting the names of all the streets," Ky laughed. "You want to talk on the doorstep? We're just standing around,"

So we both sat down and talked and talked.
I didn't get to see his mom or Hailey, but, well, I was fine with just him.

Chapter 8

Kylen

BECKETT: What about your house, anyway? Is he the son of a police officer or something lol

should I be worried?

?????

VAL: Why dont you just go down and ask him the next time he comes

how the heck am I supposed to do that???

BECKETT: It's no biggie. He is probably not supposed to be snooping around other's business simply like that. Why don't you go down, ask for his name, and ask what he's doing?

I think maybe I'll ignore him after all.

VAL: KY, YOU ARE GOING OUT THERE AND YOU ARE GOING TO TALK TO HIM. YOU HEAR ME?

I don't want tooooooooooooooo

PIXIE: Don't be stupid. Just go already

VAL: Ky, this is your house! You have all rights to ask him! If you say something wrong, just apologise and start again! You can do this, Ky. We all believe in you! <3

I think I can do it.

BECKETT: Aw yah man, that's the spirit

PIXIE: Bro got zero social skills

I was literally shaking in my socks when I looked through my window. There was the boy, examining my house up and down. I could tell from his appearance that he was about the same age as me. How was I going to start the conversation?

After brushing my hair super-quick to not look like a scrappy kid who'd escaped a zombie apocalypse, I padded down the staircase. I put on some scruffy old flip-flops and peeped through the doorhole. *Shoot.* He was still there.

I opened the door as slowly as possible, straightening my olive-green sweater with one hand. I stepped out awkwardly as if I'd forgotten which arm had to swing with each leg. Thank goodness the ginger-haired boy was still immersed in his notebook, balancing it on the fence.

Then I saw it was not a notebook but a sketchbook. He was scribbling something in it, not even noticing I was standing like a deer in headlights.

But then the boy looked up straight, surprised upon seeing me. My heart beat faster, realising I didn't rehearse what I would say. I blinked cluelessly, trying to remember why I was there.

"H-hallo," I squeaked, staring at the boy awkwardly. "Um…"

The boy grinned at me with a sheepish look, giving me a small, bright wave. "Hi,"

"Uhh, sorry to interrupt, uh, whatever you're doing right now," I rubbed the back of my neck. "But, uh, why are you, uh, always hanging around my house?"

"Oh!" the boy bit his lip sheepishly. "Um, well, you can come over here and see for yourself," the boy said, flipping the pages of his sticker-filled sketchbo-

-ok. I came closer, the colourful sketches on the pages making me curious on what they were.

I couldn't help but feel I'd known him from somewhere…

Standing beside him, I saw that he was awfully talented at artwork. He'd sketched down my house roughly with bright colours, like the kind you see in children's books.

"*No*. You did *not* just draw that," I blinked in surprise.

"Well, I did," the boy chucked softly. "Most don't believe it until I show them how I do it. It's as if artists do not exist at all on planet Earth or something,"

I chuckled too. I glanced up at him and saw his face properly- he did look rather familiar.

He had brown freckles and sort of tousled, fluffy ginger hair.

"So I drew your house from a bird's perspective, like, if this was a picture taken on a camera, it would be up there- perhaps on the electricity lines, see?" he explained with enthusiasm.

"Oh, yeah," I looked up, trying to process what the boy meant.

"Usually, one would want to draw a subject from the exact point of view they have of it, but I find it hard

to replicate it exactly, so I imagine a new perspective
and draw a couple of rough lines to form cubes and
spheres, adding extra elements, like plants, after the
base sketch is done," the boy went on, then paused.
"Wait, do I make any sense?" he asked, looking rather
anxiously at me.
"You do, you do, in a way," I said with a grin. "I love
your artwork,"
"Aw, thanks. I love drawing, and I'm thinking of
making a career out of it," the boy chuckled shyly.

"Oh, that sounds cool," I gave him a slight grin.
"What job are you planning to get?"

"Perhaps an animator. Or a writer. Maybe a children's
illustrator. A voice actor, perhaps I'd go for
designing… but I really haven't decided on one thing
yet. How about you?"
"I want to become a photographer, maybe a librarian.
Or… I'm really not sure. I usually tell everyone that I
want to become a doctor just to impress them, but I
have a feeling that's not what I want to be,"

"Ah, I feel that way a lot. My parents asked me to tell
other people I wanted to be a physician, but I'd never
want to leave art for that, though it's a great professio-

-n," the boy looked sympathetic.
"Oh, and what's your name?"

"I'm Kylen," I said, quicker than intended.
"Ky?" the boy blinked in surprise, pausing. "Oh, uh, my name is Eli,"

Eli. *Eli?*
"Ahhh, I seeee," I stretched, biting my lip. I realised why he looked so familiar. "Eli Wind?"

"Yeah," he said quietly. I could literally see the bulb in his head light up.

I might as well been melting into honey then.

Chapter 9

Eli

Oh, la, la, I feel oh-so happy.
Like I could do a little tappy—
Tappity tap around my home
Spinning around my garden gnome
I could bear my sibling's annoying pleas
And play with her and her toys with ease

Eat all the knowledge in my books
Brush the dust off crannies 'n nooks
Have some tea on the nearby brook
Cut out stuff for my scrapbooks

It occurs to me that I'm a rubbish poet
I'll crumple this up 'n I shall throw it
Perhaps in the wastebin
Or in my file made'o tin

I do not have a file made'o tin
So where else shall I chuck it in?
What am I going on about? I don't know
I don't suppose I will throw

That was idiotic, wasn't it?
Well, let's face it, I'm terrible at writing- be it stories
or poetry.
Maybe if I make more time, I may improve.

I was spinning around the spinny chair in my room.
It was given to me temporarily- my dad was going to
take it as soon as he came back from sailing.
Somehow I'd found the energy to clear out ten boxes
today. My mom came in earlier and gasped in surprise
at how much I'd gotten done in less than three
hours.
"Not everyday we see this much improvement, Eli,"
she nodded appreciatively and went out again

I cleared up a desk and put out a paper and pencil from my backpack. Usually, I doodle something to relax, but nothing came to mind. Maybe it was because the memory of meeting Ky earlier today was going on and on in my head, not finding an end. He's grown taller.

Do you ever have that feeling when you meet a person after a long time when you see how much they've changed and you can't believe it?

I went on and on about to my mom after coming home.

"-He looks so grown up now, Mom, and he's *tall!* I mean, he was taller than me even back then, but now he's taller! I thought I'd caught up to him by now-"

"Eli. What're you expecting? Look at yourself- he's not the only one who's grown. Don't be daft- it's only natural for teenagers to grow. You can't possibly expect him to stay the same!" she sighed heavily as she put away her clothes in her closet. "You keep going on about it,"

"Well! Am I not allowed to?" I'd pouted jokingly.

She was surprised to hear that Eli and his family were here and asked a lot of questions.

And here I am now, spinning in my spinny chair,

hugging Floppy tightly.

"Hey, Floppy's mine!" lilted a little kid behind the door.

"So what if she's yours? I can hug her, too," I stuck out my tongue.

"You can't! You're squashing her," she frowned and yanked Floppy by the ears.

"I am not! You're hurting her ears,"

"She can't feel her ears,"

"Why?"

"Because I say so,"

"Ah," I let go of Floppy, and Eliza flounced off to leave the room, but not before peeking in again.

"Boys don't hug plushies," she tilted her head, hands on her hip.

"*I* do," I grinned. "Besides, George Pig is always hugging Mr Dinosaur, isn't he?"

"Oh, yeah," she grinned back but looked thoughtful.

"But you're grown up,"

"I am. Is there a problem with that?"

"No,"

"Soo?"

"Okay, okay, I got it," Eliza whistled cheekily.

"So unfair you can whistle, and I can't," I pouted

jokingly.

"Why don't you try?" she teased.

"Y'know I can't do that,"

"Do it," she insisted.

I sighed and let out a screechy owl noise—nothing at
all like a whistle—as Eliza squealed with laughter,
scurrying all the way to Mom to tell her what had
happened. No, it's true. I can't whistle for my life.
I couldn't help but grin. Eliza could be very adorable.

I decided the paper wasn't going to be filled, today. I
didn't have a single idea to put down on it. So I spun
around again, making myself really dizzy. Bad idea.
I flopped on the bed, completely surrounded by
random clothing and started thinking.

Me and Kylen first met when we were about nine. He
was very shy back then (and he still is). He wasn't
included much in the games he played with a bunch
of other kids and was sitting alone. I joined him and
asked him for his name. And then we started talking
for a long while and I didn't want to go home. But we
had to.

We borrowed books from each other.

We played with Lego.

We had sleepovers.

We'd pretended we were in a Spider-Man story.

We shared secrets.

We texted each other with our parent's phones.

We joked, we boogied, we sang, and we wrote stories together.

I still have all the stories with me. They're very cringe-worthy, but they're all important to me.

I asked Ky if he still remembered Klay and Elmo, *Kraken Heroes.*
He said they still lingered in his head.

I can't think of anything else besides seeing him again.
I have a lot of things to tell him. A lot of things to
show him, too.

Ky *this*, Ky *that*...

Suddenly, I found myself cleaning my room faster.
I'm still at it, even as I'm writing this.
I won't have much time to spare for fun if I don't
hurry up.

Chapter 10

Kylen

Even if Val and Beckett are gone, and I haven't heard a word from Pixie, I'm still happy.

I've made a page in my scrapbook for each of them in my spare time.
For Pixie, I used a yellow page and yellow tape, Sabrina Carpenter lyrics on dried paper dipped in tea, a little drawing of her in biro, charms, and stickers to decorate. For Val, I used a violet page with olive green tape, a drawing of her, little sticky notes with random quotes, and cutouts of musical instruments from random magazines.
I made Beckett's with a red page with blue, striped tape, cutouts of skateboards and Dart Prozone's movie posters from newspapers, football stuff, and sports quotes. I made a page for myself, too.

I'm going to make one for Eli soon.

Y'know, I'm just going to dump some random bit of my memories here because it would make me feel better and heard a bit.

I've always felt a certain way since I was ten years old. There were a couple of kids in my old neighborhood who I played with.
Even if we all played together and made a good team in lock and key, I was always excluded from the conversations. It felt horrible back then to know that nobody really liked me. It was so strange that I liked all of them. I can't see why, though. They were weird and acted all grown up. I can't remember it all thoroughly.
 But I felt like I wasn't as good as I thought. Like a melted ice cream. They planted all these thoughts in my head, and I admit that traces of them still linger.

Why was I so *different?* Why did everyone seem five feet taller than me, even when I was usually the tallest in the room? Why did I never find anyone who truly wanted to be my friend?
I was given looks and stares for being a silly kid.
It hurts when you think of how many times you're asked to stop acting like a little kid, even when you *are* one.

I wondered why I didn't turn out like the others.
Now I don't any longer—my new question is why
they turned out like that in the first place.
I would often echo in my head the remarks kids made
about me often.

"Who likes a kid who doesn't play video games, eat
junk, or watch all the newest movies?"
"Who likes a kid who spends his time reading Enid
Blyton, eating fruit, and climbing trees?"
"Who likes a kid who still likes ball pits, chocolate
milk, and Paw Patrol?"
Hm.
I do.
And it was this kid.

When are ya free?

Around 5?

Sounds okay!
I have so many things to show you, and
I'm so, so excited!

I'm excited, too!

My house is a mess– I hope you
don't mind.

Wait, seriously? You told me that day
that only your room was a mess.

It was. But not any more.
I cleaned it

I should take notes from you, Eli- you're way too fast.

Like Sonic

WAIT, you still like Sonic the Hedgehog?

You don't...?

WELL, OF COURSE I STILL DO

I still do, too!! That's amazing- I thought you grew out of it or something!

Some things you don't grow out of. Sonic- never

I know! Also, my mom's calling me for lunch.

Then, when five o'clock inched closer, I put away my charms, stickers, and crafty thingamajigs.
I thought of just wearing anything, but it's my best friend, whom I'm meeting again, after two years at that. So I wore my favourite olive green hoodie. I have a lot of olive green stuff. It's my colour.

Then I told my mum. She said okay. I pulled a backpack over my shoulder, filled with scrapbooks, old writing, and photographs. I walked on the pavement and noticed the trees, sprawling and spindly, tall and ordinary.
My eyes scanned the typical houses and the limited greenery until a tree with a pint of neon orange caught my eye. I craned my head to see whatever that blazing colour was and gasped.
"Eli?"

"Oh! Hi, Ky!"

I couldn't hold back a grin. "Whatever are you doing up there?"

"What, you don't know that I like climbing trees?"

"Ah, I do, but… but it's dangerous?"

"What, we're not *nine* anymore. We can very well climb trees without falling off," Eli laughed.

I remember when we climbed trees together and never fell once, but Eliza once had. It all seems too rose-tinted for me to handle. I forgot I had such memories in the first place, as the bad ones constantly fogged my head.

"Like we used to, hm?" I chuckled back.

"Yeah. Hey, why don't you come on up?"

"...What?"

"*Psh, psh, psh,* climb up," he tutted impatiently, gesturing me to come up.

"Seriously?"

"I am very much, indeed, serious," Eli said in a funny voice.

I couldn't help but laugh. How was it that he was still so silly?

"It's been a while since I've climbed trees," I replied drily.

"I'm sure you still can. You're not an *old man*. I'll give you a hand,"

"Wait, how?"

"I'll just bend over like this-"

"NO, DON'T. You'll fall over," I exclaimed. "I'll… I'll come up,"

And I glanced at the sort of old trunk, looking for any loose bugs. There weren't any. So I heaved onto the part where the trunk separated into three strong branches. I held a sturdy, smaller one to pull myself up. Now, I was up on the tree, next to Eli, swinging our legs without a word.

"How are we going to get down?" I asked.

"No idea. I guess we jump,"

"Huh? You sure?" I blinked.

"It's the only way," Eli nodded with a deadpan face.

"You can't be serious. We're pretty high up here," I raised an eyebrow.

"You tell me a better idea,"

"If you don't know how to get down, why'd you even come up here in the first place?"

"Why'd you come up with me, then?"

"Cause you asked! I guessed you knew!"

"I said we could jump!" Eli laughed. It was not funny.

"I'm going down," I huffed, lowering a foot onto a smaller branch. Ah, it wasn't strong enough! It is bent scarily. I lifted my foot back up.

"Oh, dear," Eli bit his lip. "How are you going to get down, then?"

Agh. If I couldn't get down, that meant Eli couldn't either. So I thought for a moment.

"I'll try jumping down," I said but hesitated. The ground looked so far…

"Hey, you can do it. The tree's not too high, and you're tall. Just imagine you're Spider-Man or something," Eli nudged me gently.

"Well," I looked down.

"I guess I could do it,"

And I landed on both feet. One foot bent a bit, but it didn't hurt too bad. I turned, looked up, and gave Eli a silly thumbs-up with both hands. He gave me one back and jumped down, too.

I wouldn't have climbed a tree again in a long while if not for the boy in the neon woolly jumper.

★★★

"KY??" Eliza squealed and ran towards us with great force. She hugged my legs tightly, almost toppling me over. Woah, the kid had grown—a lot.
Eli shook his head with a sheepish grin. We were standing in the main doorway and hadn't even walked a step further. So strange that Eliza recognised me at first sight, but neither Eli nor I could each other. Some things are never to be known.

Quaint articles were displayed on the mantle, untamed plants grew in wild directions in each corner, family pictures hung on the wall with genuine, toothy grins, and the house was beautiful with a wide, circular jute rug adorning the tidy floor.

Eli told me to sit on the teal-ish grey sofa while he fetched a glass of water. Eliza put away her books in a hurry. Then I noticed the boxes in the room were strewn about everywhere. Half the room was tidy, and the other half was a disaster. I remember Eli's house always looked very homey and aesthetic, so I didn't take much notice of it. I was sure the next time I stopped by, the house would look amazing.
The alleyway, which probably led to the bedrooms, was empty. Maybe it led to Eli's room.

Eliza finally picked up all her books and put them on the crooked bookshelf. Crookedly.

"My books are supposed to go on a different shelf, but I'm putting them here 'cause there's not enough space for me to stand in the bedroom," Eliza said sheepishly.

"Your bookshelf is in your bedroom?" I asked, wanting to hear more of her adorable, soft lilt.

"Yeah! We have five bookshelves in there!" she enthusiastically put all five fingers in my face.

"Oh, five?" that sounded like a lot of shelves to put in one bedroom…

"Yeah, I can show you if you'd like," Eliza offered.

"No chance of that, kid," Eli came in with a laugh as I straightened in surprise. "The room's in no shape to go in,"

"I'm pretty sure it's not that bad," I grinned, taking the glass of water in Eli's hand.

"Sorry I took a while to get the water- I was looking for proper glasses to fill. I had to empty a box to find these,"

"Hey, hey, that's no problem. I don't mind even drinking from a pot or something," I joked.

"That's kinda what we're doing right now," Eli said.

"Oh! I'd have never guessed,"

***"ELI!"**￼*

I almost dropped my water. Eli sighed and yelled back.

"WHAT, MUM??"

"WHO WAS THAT AT THE DOOR??"

"IT'S KY!!"

"WHO??"

Eli face-palmed. "I might go deaf at this rate," Eliza snickered.

"I'll just go to her," Eli grinned. I grinned back in amusement. I never yelled to my mom across rooms when guests were around, but Eli didn't mind little things like that. It was nice, actually. Pretty amusing. So I was with Eliza again, sitting cross-legged on the beanbag, drumming her fingers. She was SO adorable that I wanted to squash her or something. Her tiny hands, her big ol' eyes, her tidy hairdo, her little dress- I suddenly wanted a younger sister out of nowhere.

"Hey, Eliza,"

"Hm?" she looked up.

"Do you remember me?"

Eliza blinked for a moment before answering.

"I do, yeah,"

"Do you remember Kraken Heroes?"
"That silly ol' story you guys made about those weird octopus kids?"
"Ahh... right, that,"
"Yeah! Eli kept those drawings in plastic binders,"
"Oh! Does he still have them?" I asked.
"Oh, yeah! But he never lets me touch them," Eliza pouted.
"Dear, dear," I shook my head in apparent sympathy. Eliza wasn't as good as Eli at filing away things for safe-keeping, so I was secretly happy she didn't get her hands on them, however good she was.

There was a muffled commotion inside the house. I guessed it was Eli and his mum, and I was right.

"Did your mum know I was coming over?"
"No," Eliza shook her head, flattening her dress.
"Huh...? Really?" My mum wouldn't have it if we simply invited people over without her consent. It would be quite the scene.
"Yeah,"
Eliza started drumming her tiny fingers again on the beanbag in boredom while I examined the house again. I was silently waiting for Eli to come with his

mum, who would ask dozens of questions, until I burst.

Which was what happened, by the way.

Eli's mum (her name was Erica) walked to the living room with a couple of glasses filled with pink guava juice.

"Kylen, dear! Hello!" she chirped and I felt a nervous tingle grow.

"Hallo, Mrs Wind!" I grinned wider than normal.

"It's, uh, been a while, hasn't it, Mrs Wind?"

"Quite a while! How you've grown! Take this," she handed me a cup from the tray of two other cups.

"Aw, thanks, Mrs Wind," I took the glass as gently as possible. Nope, wouldn't want to topple it over like I always did.

"So? How's the new house? Settled in?" she asked warmly, sitting on the opposite side of the sofa to face me. Eli and Eliza tussled to win a seat on the beanbag as she spoke, but I pretended not to give much notice.

"The new house is very… nice, Mrs Wind. We've settled in well," 'Nice' was a word I didn't like using too often. But strangely, it was the only word that fit most things.

"Nice? Ah, I see. How's your sister?" she asked,

looking a tad less excited. Perhaps 'nice' wasn't enough of a word for her, either.

"She's doing very well, Mrs Wind," I smiled politely.

Oh, dear, was I addressing her far too much?

"She's been buried in her books for ages, though, as her new school has been taking up most of her time,"

"Oh, perhaps she needs a break, poor thing, no? How are your studies?"

Agh. Downhill. I've a lot to catch up on.

"Pretty good, Mrs Wind,"

I glanced over at Eli, who was sitting on the rug reluctantly next to a proud Eliza on her prize beanbag. Heh, sillies.

"That's good to hear. Eli has been a couple of months behind, you see. Can you help him catch up? Moving and such has taken up quite a lot of time," Mrs Wind asked as a red Eli looked up at the ceiling in embarrassment. He stood up and shifted behind the sofa arm where his mum was.

"Muuum," Eli shook her mildly, whining. "I want to spend time with himmm,"

"Oh, sorry, sorry, you kids go on, scurry scurry," Mrs Wind laughed.

Eli grinned sunnily and beckoned me to follow, earning a disapproving look from Mrs Wind. "Eli, you're not taking Kylen to your bedroom, are you?"

"He said he'll help me clean it up!" Eli hollered, pulling me through the empty alleyway that led to two doorways, one with tidily stacked boxes, otherwise clear, the other with miscellaneous tidbits of beads, pencils, stickers, books, and whatnot. Huh, strange for Eli, of all people, to have a bedroom like this. Then again, he and his mum never ceased to amaze me with their speedy cleanship, so I doubted if the room would stay this way for long.

"Ahhh, Ky, I am so sorry about this room, but you should've seen it yesterday—there were loads more boxes than what's here now," Eli chuckled sheepishly, putting his hands on his hips.
"Mhm," I nodded, taking in all the stuff on the floor. And on the bed. And on the sideboard. The only clear surfaces were in front of the bed and on an old wooden desk.
Nope. Even for me, this room was hard to clean up.

"My mum's pretty embarrassing, isn't she?"

"Huh?"
"Well, she's pretty- y'know- chatty and stuff?"
"Didn't seem too bad to me. I like her," I smiled.

I glanced at the floor.
"How are we going to clean this up?" I asked, hesitating.
"Wait, wait— *we?*" Eli looked up from the floor.
"You're seriously going to help me?"

Oh. So he thought I was joking.
"Of course I am," I grinned. "Some music would help,"
"That we can do," Eli smiled back, taking his phone to put on a track. "What song?"
"Anything by Madilyn Mei,"

We made a lot of progress, and oh, was it hard work, folding, separating, lifting, discarding- but doing it together— that made it all the better.
Do you know that feeling when you spend time with someone you care about? When you get a feeling in your heart, like some golden light?
I still had it for the rest of the day.

Chapter 11

Eli

Eliza is not only jealous but also very, very unhelpful. First of all, why is she jealous? It's because I have a friend, and she does not (not yet, anyway, because the girl next door doesn't appeal to her too much).

She was mad 'cause I shooed her out of the room. Why? I've an excellent reason. First of all, it was *my* room (and it is not her business to snoop in without permission), and it was my friend she was hogging all the time. I tried telling her, hey, it's been TWO YEARS SINCE I'VE PROPERLY SPOKEN TO MY FRIEND, and it was so unfair of her to come and butt in our discussions, but she doesn't seem to get it.

I'd invited Ky over earlier today, and we climbed a tree, blah, blah, some stuff happened, and now we were cleaning my room together.

"Hey, Eli," Ky called, sitting on the floor opposite me, organising Lego.

"Hm?" I looked up.

"Do you still draw Kraken Heroes?"

"Oh, of course, yeah," I laughed. "I mean, it was fun writing it. And I still like the story, but it's weird, with kids with Kraken power thingies and stuff, alternative dimensions, hm-hm," I did a so-so gesture with a grin.

"We sure can do a better job when we rewrite that," *When* we rewrite that- not *if*- which meant he was up for it. Wow.

"And we can change the silly names," I said.

Ky grinned at that. "I kinda got attached to Klay and Elmo. I don't think I want to change it,"

"Me neither," I grinned back. "After the house is set, I'll call you over to rewrite it,"

"Huh?? Really?"

"Of course, silly,"

"Woaw. That sounds great," Ky glowed. "Brings back old times. I think Klay and Elmo were made, like, four years back?"

"That's a long time. I didn't realise they were that old- *hey, stop!*"

Ky was absentmindedly pouring down a box of just tidied Legos.

Ky and I exchanged glances.

"Uugghhhh," we groaned and started over.

"I've been doing a lot of writing in between," Ky began after a moment. "My mom loves that I do, so she prompts me a lot,"

"Hm?" I looked up in interest. "What kind of stories?"

Ky was always good at cooking up stuff. I loved reading his work- maybe he could've became an author someday.

"I started out small with animals and insects and gave them cute names and personalities. Then I did a couple one-shots of school stories. Some about fantasy, too. I could show you," he said, his face lighting up a bit after I'd asked.

"Yeah, definitely!" I paused. "Well, one day," I added, taking a look at my room. This was never ending.

"Maybe I'll stop by to help you now and then,"
"Seriously?" I raised an eyebrow in astonishment.
"Can you do that?"
"I'll ask my mom. If she says I can, I'm here,"
"Hey that's awesome!"
"I know!"
And that's when Eliza barged in.
"What're you laughing about?" she asked in interest, plopping in between us.
"Ky says he'll come over when he's free to help us

clean up!" I chirped.

"Us? You mean with *your* room? Nobody's bothered about me or *my* room,"

"Oh, dear. Eliza, I'd love to see your room," Ky said quickly, so as to not hurt her feelings.
Agh. This was Eliza's cue to start chatting nonstop all the way.

"This is my room. It's very neat," she gave me a look. Yeah, yeah, it was neat cause she dumped all the 'messy' stuff in *my* room.
"It's not finished yet. These are my bookshelves, but they needs to be fitted. And this," she stopped, posing dramatically "Is my table,"
"Woah. I loved how nicely you decorated it!" Ky gave her a appreciative smile. Eliza smiled back widely, giggling.
Hm. Perhaps Ky would be a far better brother than I was. I had to step up my game, then.
"This is all the stuff in my closet. It's a mess," she added sheepishly, as numerous plushies fell out as she opened it.
Eliza! I thought you'd cleaned that, you booger!" I hissed. Most definitely, it was going to lead up to me

cleaning it up, following with Eliza using her lame old excuse of not knowing *how* to clean it up.

"Remind me why I'm here," Ky grinned, a little uneasily.
"Ky! No way are you helping with *this*," I exclaimed indignantly.
Ky sighed. "Yeah, a little overambitious, mm?"
"It's already too much with you doing so much help," I laughed. "Let's take a break or something,"
"It's no problem," he shook his head, smiling at the suggestion cheerily. "We could get some water,"

***

We made our way to the kitchen. I felt super-guilty for how the house was, but I decided not to make that a big problem. I picked up the glasses I'd used earlier and rinsed them, filling them with water to hand to Ky and to Eliza.

"I'm sorry we haven't much to eat- we're out of snacks," I said, sipping my water.
"No problem," Ky shook his hand. Still, it was unfair that I invited him over and didn't give him anything to eat.
"We've got way too many fruit, though! How about

an apple?" I suggested.

"That sounds nice. I like fruit," Ky shrugged, smiling dorkily. Eliza asked for an apple, too.

So when I insisted I sliced the apples on my own, Ky gave up on trying to help and went to the living room, chattering with Eliza.
I put all the pieces in a white bowl and made my way to the half-cleaned living room. My mom had gone out for a walk, so the house was to ourselves, although not in its best state.

"Ky," I asked after pondering on what to talk about. "Have you… like, made any friends, here?"
"Friends?" Ky looked up from his fidgeting fingers. "I do, uh, have three friends. Val, Pixie, and Beckett,"
"Wow, that's, that's great!" I sputtered. "How are they? To you, I mean? Are they nice?"
"They're great. They're cool. But… sometimes I feel like the odd one out since I'm the only awkward one in the group, but… uh, it's not too bad since they accept me and stuff," Ky said in a matter-of fact tone with gaps in between. "Well… Sometimes I wonder if they just bear with me and don't really like me, y'know, like they're too nice to try ditching me-" I put up a hand in his face to stop him.

Ky flinched a little when I did that, but he calmed when he saw my expression.

"Don't say that. I'm sure they like you, Ky. You're amazing," I said, lowering my hand as Eliza shuffled beside me, reaching to the wooden table to pick up an apple slice. "You're just… shy, I guess. But you're cool,"

Ky smiled shyly. "Well, you're cooler,"

"Nah, no way, buddy," I chuckled. "You get that title, not me. Tell me more about your friends,"

"Well, best of all, there's Valencia Garcia. She's my friend from school. And without her, I don't suppose school would be as easy to go through. We all call her Val. She's awesome and plays electric guitar, even trying to compose her own songs! Val is super-kind and supportive. Since she befriended me, Pixie came as a part of the package. Pixie's spunky and possessive, but she can be a sport. I don't know much about her, though. Beckett is my neighbor. He's pretty chill, but he's the typical boy- video games, football, and such- but he's nicer than most," Ky went on and on about his friends and how they got along.

I was happy for him, but… I felt odd.

Although his descriptions of his friends and the stories he told of them seemed totally positive, how come I didn't like them at all? It was great that Ky wasn't lonely anymore, but I felt like my spot was taken. No place for me.
It was supposed to be 'Ky and Eli', not 'Ky's bunch of of friends and some old friend that isn't relevant to the plot'.
Urgh. I just pretended I never felt that. I was being unreasonable.

But one thing I knew for sure- you can't trust your feelings to follow what your head says.

Chapter 12

Kylen

"Ky!" my mom called from the kitchen.

"WHAT?!" I yelled back, my throat croaking a little. Then she yelled back again, but I didn't understand what she yelled.

"MOM, I CAN'T HEAR YOU,"

Then my mom said something in vague and warbled gibberish that I couldn't make out, not from my bedroom, anyway.

"Urgh," I climbed off my flompy bed, dropping stickers and notes to the floor. "Oh, dear," I picked them up. I wouldn't want them to get lost under the bed and find their way to the bin.

"KYLEN SCOTTS!!"

I didn't feel like yelling back, so I ran down as quickly as possible before she yelled out my name another time.

"It's too bad we have a first floor here. Perhaps I would've been more *audible* if your room was on the same floor," Mom groaned, pinching between her eyebrows. "Why did you not wash the dishes? Why do you come and dump all your dirty plates and mugs and never *flinch* when you know you're shoving all this to me? When do you plan to clean all this?"

I pursed my lip. I was so into making that scrapbook page for Eli that I disregarded almost all my chores. Oh, dear, I was in for a telling-off.

"It's great and all for you to be on school holidays, but that doesn't mean discipline is off the chart. Look at me. Look at your sister. She hasn't seen the daylight for days, poring on her books. We're both working hard. What are you doing, simply leaving us to do all the washing up? Can't you do a *single thing* in the house for our sakes?" she ranted on and on, and I didn't say a word. I felt awful about it, and I started washing hurriedly as she continued.

"...you expect us to help you when you invite your friends over, although you can very well do it yourself. Sure, I don't mind helping you host them at all- in fact, I'm happy to do it- but you have to understand how hard it is to do all the housework, take care of you both, go to work, and barely manage to take time for myself! Are you even listening?”

“Yes, Mom,” I croaked.

“You haven’t a word to say, hm? I haven’t even heard a sorry from you,”

“I’m sorry,”

“Tch,” Mom sighed heavily in frustration. “That’s all I can expect from you, anyway,”

So, I was left to do the dishes in the full sink. This was a simple job, which I should’ve done earlier. Then there wouldn’t be such a load to wash.

The words my mom said stung because it was true. I haven’t been the most responsible lately, and my head has been in a fog. As a very organised person, I was the least organised one around.

As I scrubbed the plates free of pasta stains and whatnot, I thought of my scrapbook page.

It wasn’t the most productive thing in the world, but I loved making it. My mind wandered to the little important things I put together- a little poem, a couple of old photographs, cutouts, and little charms… I wanted to go back and finish them. I wished I could use my camera, but there were still four days until my camera ban expired. Ah, well. Ugly photos on my old phone had to do for printing out.

Sometimes, a scrapbook is like a visual journal. Or an abstract image of a feeling, person, object, place.
It's… really… hm, how should I put it…
It's makes me feel at peace and I express myself through it.
I sighed, seeing the rest of the dishes in the sink. Not too many, though, but it would take me a little longer.
Scrub, scrub, wash, wash… Mom was right. If I'd done this earlier, there wouldn't be this much to wash up anyway.
So, to make the washing a little more enjoyable, I put on an indie radio on my phone and set it down on the counter.
"Run, go back to your home
History is no one's friend
Now, you'll never be known
As only Joan again
As only Joan again-"
Ping!

"Huh?" I turned around. My phone screen was lit, showing a notification of a text.

Must've been a picture or two from Val. She always

sent me pictures of whatever was going on- in this case, probably her cousin's wedding.

So I went back to the dishes, humming a tune.

When I finished up and dried my hands with a dish towel, I opened my phone.

There was a text from a contact with a Fluttershy profile picture.

Pixie?

This was totally out of the blue. She almost never texted me. Perhaps here and there, she would send photos of us having shaky selfies together and ask us what time we were hanging out, but that was mostly in the group chat.

Whatever was it?

I opened the notification, and it turned out that Pixie had sent me a document.

Bday Invit.2

Huh?

Under the document, Pixie had sent me a text.

Huh?

I opened the document, and it appeared to be a digital

invitation.

And when I read who it was from, I couldn't help but gasp aloud.

That was pretty corny for someone like Shanelle.
Agh. There was no way I was going.
Sure, it may be fun, but for me? I was never one for crowded parties.
Or unwanted conversation.
Or… for feeling like an outsider.

She didn't answer right away like she always did. I sure hoped she saw it soon since the party was the day after tomorrow.
I went back upstairs, opening my treasured scrapbook again. Huh, I'd done a pretty good job on the page. I just needed one more print of a photograph…
Shoot. I'd left my phone downstairs.
I groaned and sped downstairs, nearly tripping on the cloud-shaped mat on my way to the little kitchen.
And as I'd anticipated, there was a text from Pixie.

Okay, so I wasn't expecting that. Why *me?*
But I didn't ask. I typed the best answer I could think of.

I had to tell my mom about this party, or else I might not go. I stepped downstairs as slowly as possible. I sure hoped she'd ask me to stay home and do some work or something. I felt a bit small for giving up so quickly on my will to Pixie. I should've just put my phone down and ignored her. But that would've been mean…

"Sure, you can go, Kaley," my mom said cheerily.
Huh??
"Mom, really? But Shanelle-"
"She's invited you, no?"
"Mom! Pixie's invited, not me. And she's calling me only 'cause Shanelle has allowed the guests to bring someone along. If Val was here, I was never an option,"
"Ahh, yes, I see, kiddo," she ruffled my hair affectionately.
"Shanelle isn't my favourite either. But you can't stay inside forever. Go out for a bit and talk to new people! Do it for your friend at least. For me. It's awful seeing you always cooped up in your room like your sister,"

And I knew there was no arguing with her.

I mean, Shanelle wasn't too bad, but I didn't like her.

Everything she said or did has a tinge of red in it.

Did she give you a compliment? Did she help you
with setting up your locker? Does she talk sweetly to
you? She's only being friendly to you cause you're the
one with the secrets she wants to gossip about.

Okay, that *is* very, very bad.

I just hope Pixie isn't as dense as I was.

School is going to be a prison yard otherwise.

Chapter 13

Eli

Eliza was one fly I couldn't shoo and one tiger I couldn't make see sense.

"RAWRRR," Eliza yelled in my ear.

"RAAAWWWRRR," I roared in her face. "Go do some work. Clean your room or something," I said as I slumped in my spinny office chair.

"Work is boring," Eliza jumped in my lap. Agh, a few years ago, this would've been quite cosy. Now, I was having a heavy, tall kid clambering all over me.

"Get off, kid," I grumbled under the pile of bones.

"No,"

I picked her up. She was pretty heavy, too. So I plopped her on my floral-patterned bed.

"Hey! That's rude," she grumbled.

"I'm calling Ky over again today, Eliza, so be good and don't interrupt," I said as firmly as I could, but Eliza didn't like that.

"Well, I'll tell Mum you're not including me," she pouted.

"Hah, whatever. You have that girl who lives across

us for company,"
"Shambhavi? She talks too much. If she starts, she never stops," she gave the bed a little bounce.
"Sounds familiar," I said, holding back a wide grin.
"Huh? What do you mean?"
"Nothing," I shrugged.
She eyed me suspiciously and walked out of the room.
"I'm going out to play!" she exclaimed in the alleyway excitedly.
I knew she would like little Shambhavi eventually. I liked her very much. She'd come over to give us a bowl of kaju katlis. They were really yum, and I don't think a kid who makes sweets with her mum could be that annoying like Eliza said.

I checked my phone. I looked out the windows.
No sign of Kylen Scotts. Not a peep from him.
Well, he did say something like he had a birthday party he didn't want to go to.
I figured he'd not go, but it turns out I was wrong.
Oh, well. I was looking forward to him meeting my dad, who's supposed to be here later today. That's one plus less, so I thought of curling up in bed and reading something good to make up for the sad disappointment.

Some cookies would be nice to go with it.

Or I could go out with Eliza. It's been a while since I've gone out and I haven't seen much of our neighbours. The only kids I've met so far are Ky and Shambhavi. So I decided to put on some cool clothes and my new pair of fluorescent kicks. They're very cool and make me feel like Miles Morales a bit.

I closed my door with a quiet creak after I told Mum I was going out. It seemed to have rained earlier, which was strange since it had been sunny a lot lately. Too sunny- that's why I wasn't out too much. The grass was sort of damp which wasn't so good for my shoes, so I went as slowly and carefully as I could with them. I did good on that until Eliza darted right into me.

"URRRGH, ELIZA," I squealed. "WHY,"

So my shoes were in a bad state, i.e. totally covered in mud, and I was nearly in tears- and my sister was totally in my bad books- no- worst books, to say the least.

"Shambhavi pinched me!" Eliza whined.

"You're being silly," I groaned. "Why did she pinch you?"

"Because I wore my shoes in her house. It's such a

silly reason, too,"
Why she was trying to find so much fault in
Shambhavi, I didn't know.
"Maybe she *doesn't* wear shoes in her house. I mean,
just look at your crocs- they're so muddy and
everything. You certainly deserved that,"
"Ah, yeah," she put her hands on her hip.
"But...but I don't *want* to play with her,"
"Why not? She's nice,"
"I don't like her. She's not like Avery,"
I heard a little whimper from her bent head.
"Avery?" I bent down to see Eliza's tearful face.
"Hey, hey, don't cry. Do you miss her that much?"
"Yah," she sniffed, snot in her nose a bit. "I do,"

So I wasn't the only one who missed old friends.
I tried to make her feel better with a hug, but in my
head, my thoughts were screaming louder than I
could ever.
Why is change so, *so, SO* hard to go through?!

Chapter 14

Kylen

Today was the day- the day of that horrid party. I had my clothes all ironed to a crisp. I silently wished that Val could've come earlier from her holiday. I mean, it wouldn't have had to be me that had to go if she did.

I took a deep breath. Shanelle didn't want me at her party, obviously. I could've just stayed home. It was the best decision I could think of. But heck, my mom wouldn't change her mind anytime soon, and I couldn't go back on my promise to Pixie.

I saw an image of Shanelle's house in my head. It was large and a little inaccurate to reality. Pixie and I were standing in front, all well-dressed.
We walked in. I went to the furthest corner of the crowded hall, trying to be as invisible as possible. The neon lights flecked on the number of other kids, laughing and dancing. Then a horrid, horrid thing happened.

The white light was on both Pixie and Shanelle, gaily talking to one another. It slowly, ever so slowly, started drifting my way, and soon enough, it was on me. Me, in the spotlight.

Muffled voices spoke in hushed tones.

"Nerd,"

"Loner,"

"Wimp,"

"Weirdo,"

Shanelle came to the fore and glared at me icily.

"You don't belong here. It was Pixie and Valencia we wanted, not an outsider like you,"

I froze.

Until I realized I was in my house.

In front of the mirror.

Imagining this nonsense.

Such a scene would never happen. It was far too unrealistic.

"I'll be fine," I breathed shakily in front of my reflection. "It'll all be fine. I'm just… overthinking this,"

I decided to distract myself by decorating the wrapped book and putting it in a dainty gift bag. My sister passed by my room and peeked in. Her mousy, voluminous hair was tucked in a messy bun.

"Kylen? Is that Shanelle's birthday gift?" she asked with a knowing smile.

"It's a book. *The Miscalculations of Lightning Girl*," I replied with a weak grin. "It's a goodie,"

"You think the stuck-up girl will like it?" she snickered, folding her arms casually, leaning on the door.

"I honestly don't know. I don't even think she reads," I laughed. "I don't really care, either. Never even wanted to go to this party,"

"Pixie will be ecstatic, eh?"

"Yeah… I think she still worships Shanelle," I couldn't help but laugh because isn't it funny to imagine your friend doing just that? " Well, could I blame her? Shanelle is... uh, is pretty, uh, helpful, nice, and a good listener, I guess- pretty good fashion sense, too- so-"

"Hey, hey, hey. You forgot the bit where she spreads all your secrets all over the school and talks about you behind your back and stuff,"

"Not like I didn't know that," I smirked.

"So, are you gonna rock this party or what?" Hailey said and shook me like a bottle of milk.

"What do you mean?" I said, trying to wriggle out of

her arms. "Rock" was a word I didn't go with, maybe in the context of being dull or overly kind.

"Well, what are you going to wear?"

"That," I pointed to the shirt and jeans on the bed.

"Woah, uh, you wear that all the time," Hailey scratched her head.

"Shanelle hasn't seen me wear it," I shrugged. It was a very fine shirt and I haven't spilt anything on it, thank goodness (somehow it just happens. The stain. It's very embarrassing).

"Well, I suppose. I mean, this does look very nice on you," she beamed as I went red. I don't look all too nice, in *that* shirt or any *other* shirt, but oh well. Somehow, everyone thinks otherwise.

"Aw, thanks," I said.

"No prob,"

Pixie was texting me nonstop an hour before the party.

Ky are you ready or wat

Ky answer please

So I texted her back a half-hour later.

So I was waiting on my doorstep, the little gift bag by my side. The grass was pretty wet, but the step was dry because the roof shaded it from the drizzle earlier.

Eventually, I heard a *'rrrr'* of sorts from the front of my house and I lifted my head from my knees.

It was Pixie and her mom in their little green car that can barely squash in four people, but it looked fun to go in.

And when it struck me that I actually was going to a party, probably filled with half my school, my heartbeat hitched and I became conscious of my breath.

I sure hoped nothing would go wrong.

END

Surprised by the cliffhanger
ending?
Don't worry, there'll be a book
two in 2025.
Hoped you liked it up to here!

Thank You!

Hi, hi, hi! This is the part where everyone gets their 'thank you's for helping me with this book! Without anyone's help, Ky and Eli would've stayed either as pastime drawings in my sketchbook or in an abandoned manuscript in my Google Docs. Honestly, I wouldn't have even gotten it this far without everyone's help!

The first thanks goes to my mom (who goes as Judith Woodrow and is also a writer) for sticking with me for months until I finished my book. She's always guided me through this path from my first drawing of a caterpillar when I was two. Honestly, she's my biggest inspiration. Without her, would I have really published my work, let alone have the skills to?

A big ol' THANK YOU to my sis, June, for being the proofreader even when I didn't ask her to. She's the one who gave me tons of ideas when I was stumped. Credits to June for giving me the idea of how Ky and Eli met!

She also picked out spelling errors, and it was a big bummer to see the word 'chuckled' spelt as 'chucked' on page 69 right after we ordered twenty copies. She's already told me to edit it before publishing, but I guess I forgot to. Thanks for spotting that out, bud. I also can't leave out the bit when she made me a cute fanart of Ky, even though he's super hard for her to draw! Going straight to my prized binder of fanart!

Kudos to my friends, who I'll name as Raven and Sippy (yeah, you guys are awesome), for hearing me yap on and on about my story and giving their opinions on the earlier drafts of the first two chapters. One point to Sippy for being the person who made Ky's earlier design for fun with me. Who'd've expected him to turn out to become a whole character?

A small thank you to those who inspired the creation of Shanelle, Val and Beckett, but I'm not sure they know they are the ones who I based them on. Better off not saying...

And thank YOU, the reader, for reading this book! This book that you're holding in your hands is very special to me, and I hope you find it special, too. Lots of love to you!

Zippy, a joyous zebra suitcase, finds his way to the sisters who left him behind. But the chances of not making it to the train in time are high—how is it going to work?

Read on for a peek at Ms Peanut's 5th book!

Boring as it was, I had to sit here in the closet for three whole years. Not a peep- except for the children's talk and the footsteps of their little feet.

Tiggy, my friend, sat next to me. We both watched to see if there was even a tiny twitch- a little shuffle- hoping the doors might open.

I had no idea what the date was. Or the time. It's probably a morning in June, an evening in October, or even a night in January.

But then, I heard the little twitch we'd been waiting for. The creak of the door! The giggles, the voices, oh- the doors were opening!

We were going on holiday!

Renee and Ruth, the children, packed their books, brushes, clothes, and toys into Tiggy and me. I was so excited. I saw the other boring bags with no fun designs on them. Just plain and drab, single-colored bags.

We went out the door. The bags went into the building elevator: the food bag, the laptop bag, the backpacks, Tiggy, and others. Yes, everyone- everyone but me.

Renee carried me down the stairs with Ruth a little way behind. She put me behind the five storey apartment.

The kids left- probably to get the others from the
elevator. So I waited.
I was still waiting.
Waiting. Waiting… Waitingg…
Then I got that upsetting feeling that I was left behind.
Oh, what scatterbrains the children were. They would put
shoes in the food bag, food in the laptop bag, and the
laptops in the shoe bag! And now they've put me here,
thinking the car would come in the backside.

I looked around. What funny trees! Quite many tall buildings. Lots of new faces. This was nothing like being in the closet. Time passed. I was probably standing there for like thirty minutes or so. But then I heard a clipity-clop noise. Or maybe it was a stepity-step. A kind-looking lady was talking on the phone.

"Say," she said. " Was it a zebra-like suitcase you left behind?"

NOTES FROM THE AUTHOR

So! I've finally finished the book I've been going on and on about for months together!

I've been writing and ditching multiple ideas at the double, and I couldn't finish just. One. Story.

I've been working on FOUR different manuscripts this year, and none of them are done. Even though I wrote them all with passion and high spirits. But this one? The book you're holding and are probably done with right now? The idea started with a silly doodle of an early design of Ky, made by my two good friends and me a few months before I moved. (Hi there, if you're here, guys!) Then, I developed him more and more for fun and made him all his friends, family, his home, and even the little tiny things in his room.

If we put away their similarities, Eli and Ky were supposed to be a bit like Yin and Yang. If Eli was the sunshine, Ky was the moonlight. If Eli was loud, then Ky was quiet. Extrovert, introvert. Social and shy. The list goes on. And you know what? They put together, make a <u>whole</u> me.

I've been reading a lot, experiencing a lot, and experimenting a lot while writing this. There were quite a lot of times I wanted to throw away this idea because I kept feeling I would never be good enough. But what good is it to never do it?

We'll never learn nor improve that way.

It was fun making this, and I loved giving all the characters life, but I feel that Eliza didn't get enough spotlight, so don't worry, we'll see more of her again.

I added so many things that I'd like to have myself in the background (like Val's electric guitar, Ky's entire collection of Alice Oseman's books and Sonic stuff, and Eli's house), so there was a lot of mixing in the imagination area as well as real-life scenarios (like Eli's flight trip, the broken trophy, and Ky's misadventure in the supermarket for instance).

Writing from a boy's point of view (two, to be precise) was a change for me, but I think I nailed it (sort of)- but the goal was to make them human. To make them say things I could never in real life through their stories.

So, if you've come this far in this book, wow! Why not stay longer for the next one?

Thanks for picking this book up, and keep reading!
Your pal,

Ms Peanut♥

About the Author

Ms Peanut Woodrow is a 14-year-old children's author and illustrator. She is a homeschooling girl who constantly moves around India because of her dad's transferable job and loves exploring. She loves reading children's literature and fiction and is partly inspired by the works of Jacqueline Wilson, Lauren Child, and numerous other authors and illustrators. Ms Peanut spins stories around her experiences and tales of her own life, mainly writing about friendship, family, and holidays.

She's been drawing from the moment she could hold a pencil and writing poetry and stories ever since she was a girl of 7. Ms Peanut has written and illustrated 6 books, her first one being published when she was 10, plus 2 from the Sylvia's Neighborhood series written by her younger sister, June Woodrow, all published on Notion Press and Amazon.com.

Who knows, there could be a story brewing in the mind of Ms Peanut right now...

Ms Peanut's other books:

For older readers:

1

Books by
June Woodrow
(Peanut's sister)

2